Believe in all things !

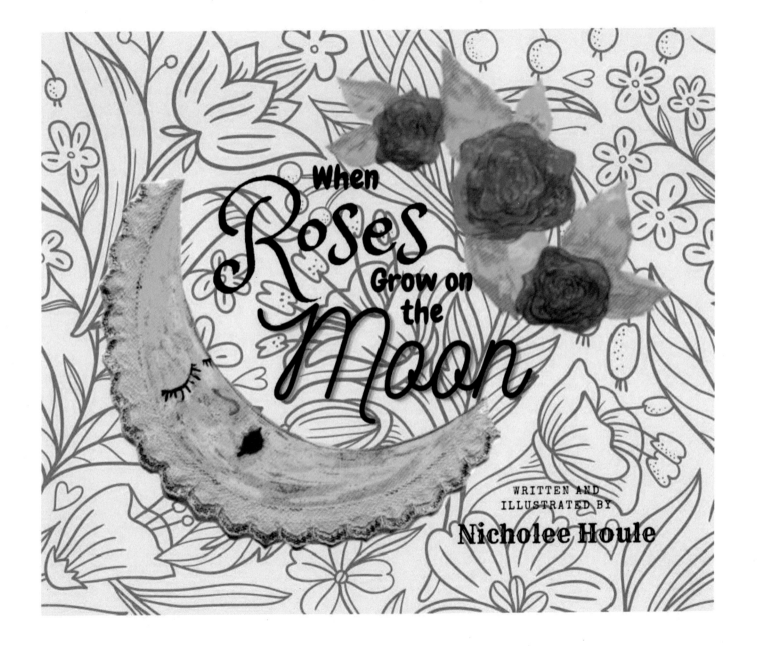

# When Roses Grow on the Moon

WRITTEN AND
ILLUSTRATED BY

## Nicholee Houle

For my Grandpa Steve.

Thank you to my dad for always believing in my poems, my mom for giving me the push to finish this book, and to my children for making me feel like a true artist.

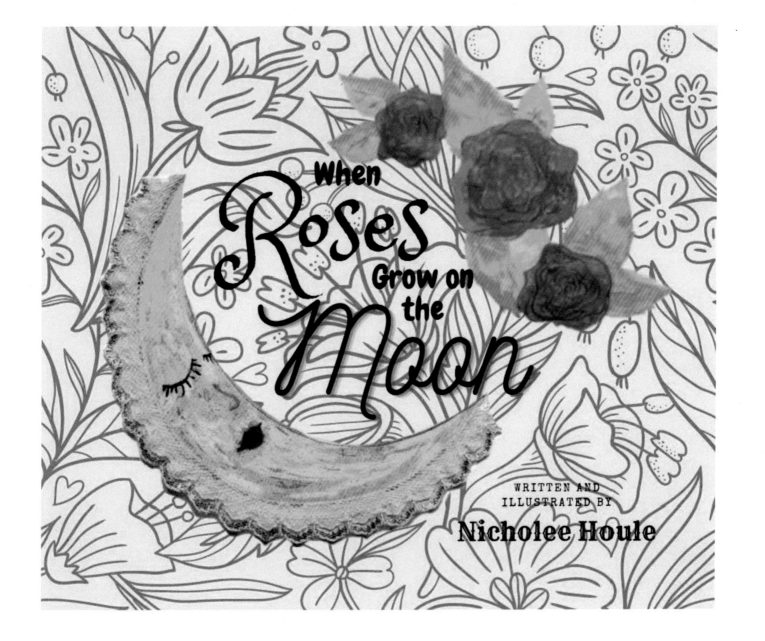

When
Roses
Grow on
the
Moon

WRITTEN AND
ILLUSTRATED BY

Nicholee Houle

Anything is possible
when roses grow on the
moon.

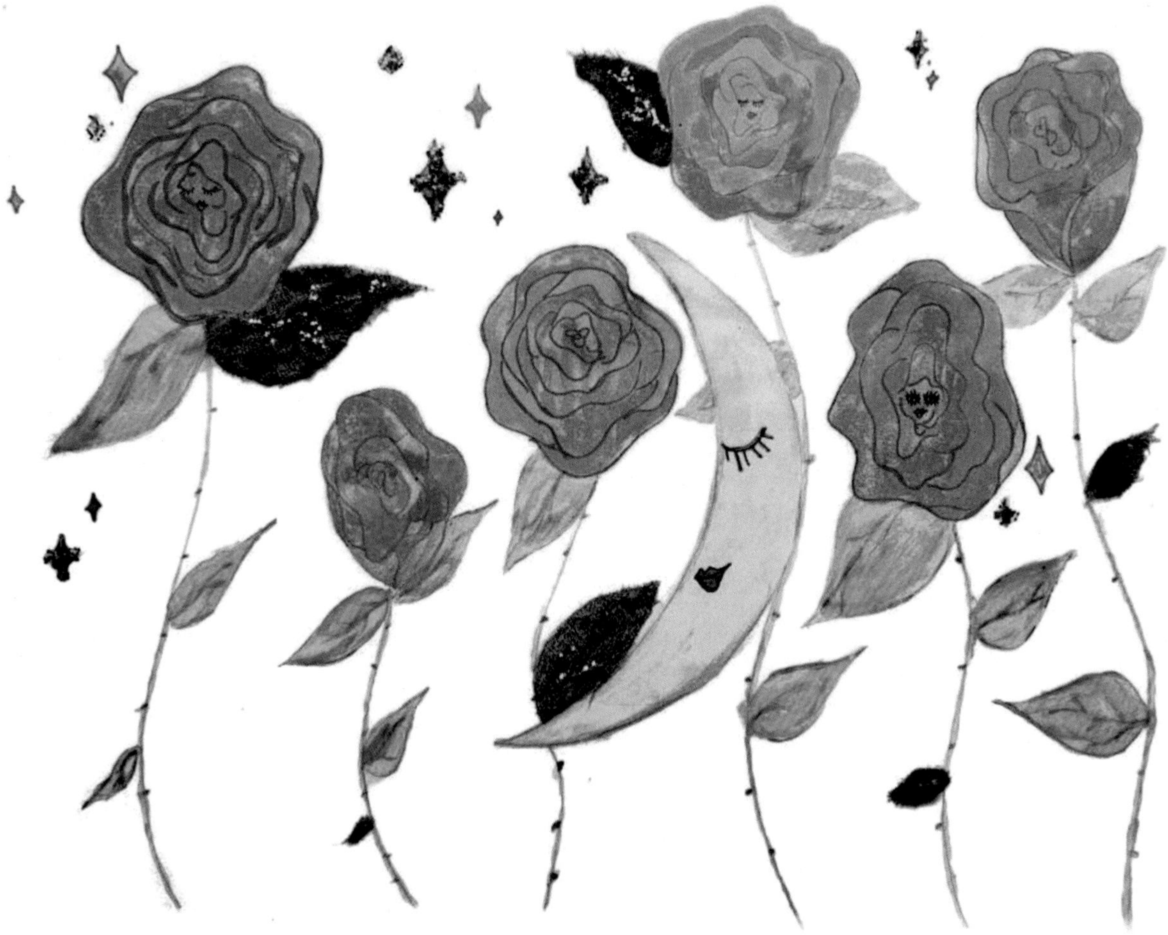

A shining girl
with golden hair could dare
to sing her tune.

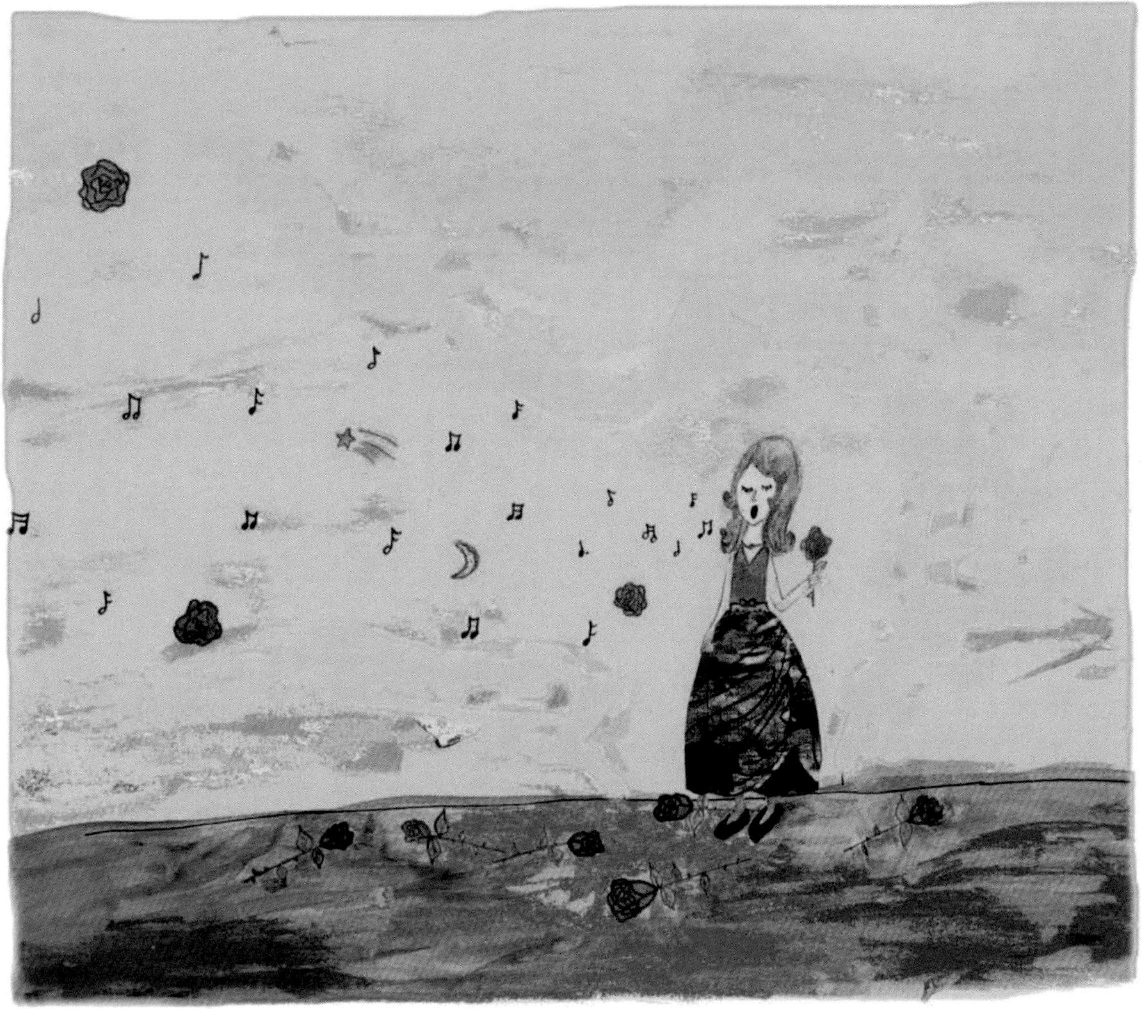

A fiery soul
with no one to tell him
could lull a lion to
sleep.

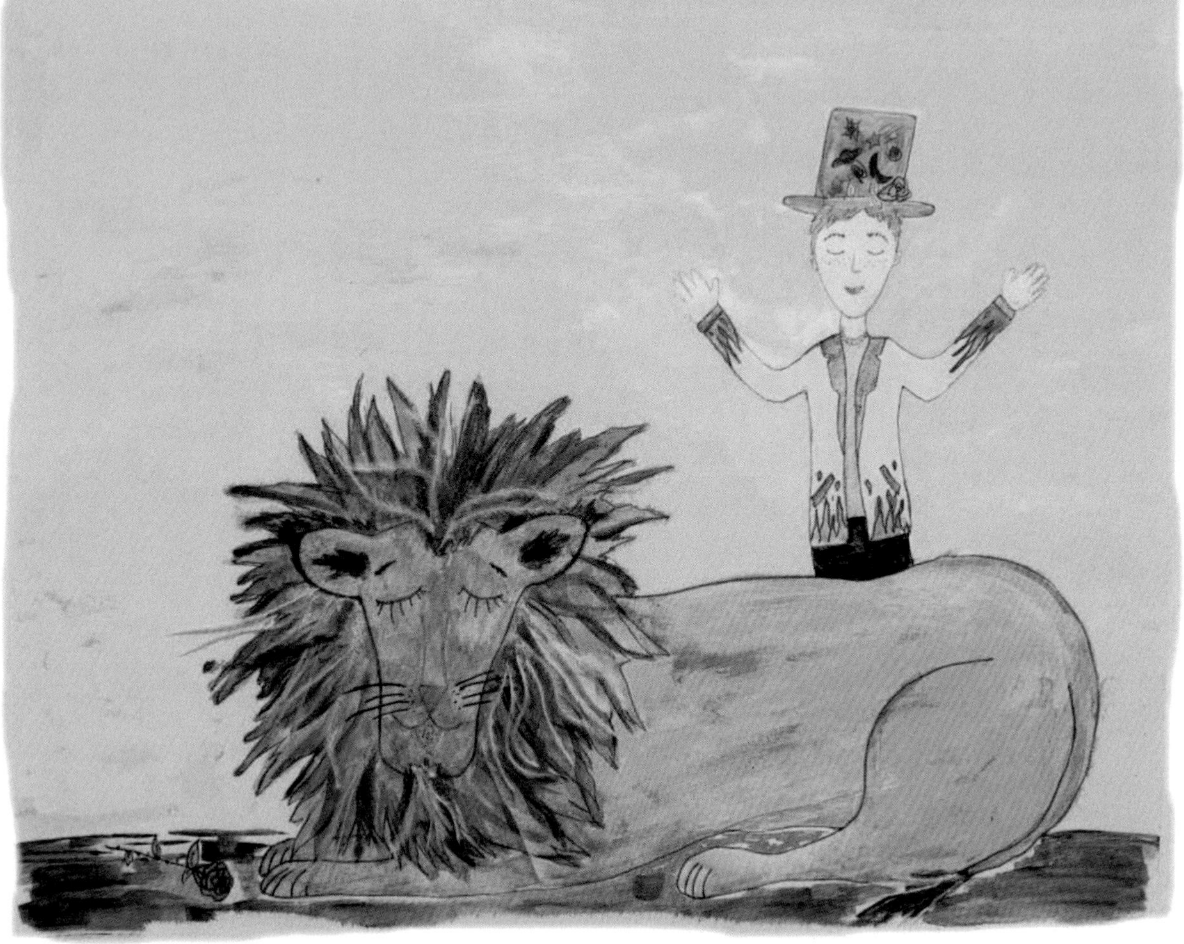

Or a timid gazer
with grounded limbs
could take her daring leap.

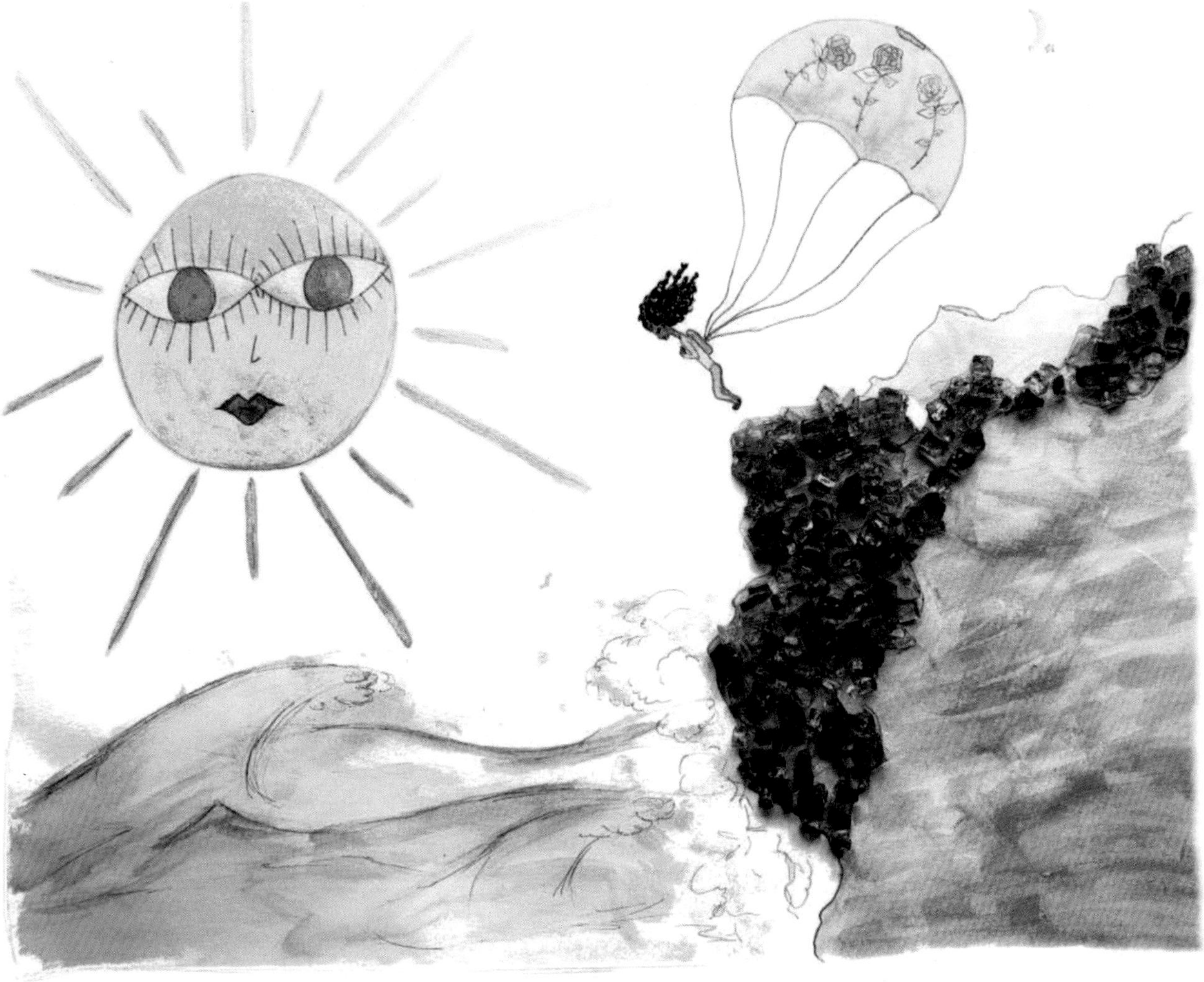

A boy who lives
in the hot summer sun
could dive to the artic
depths.

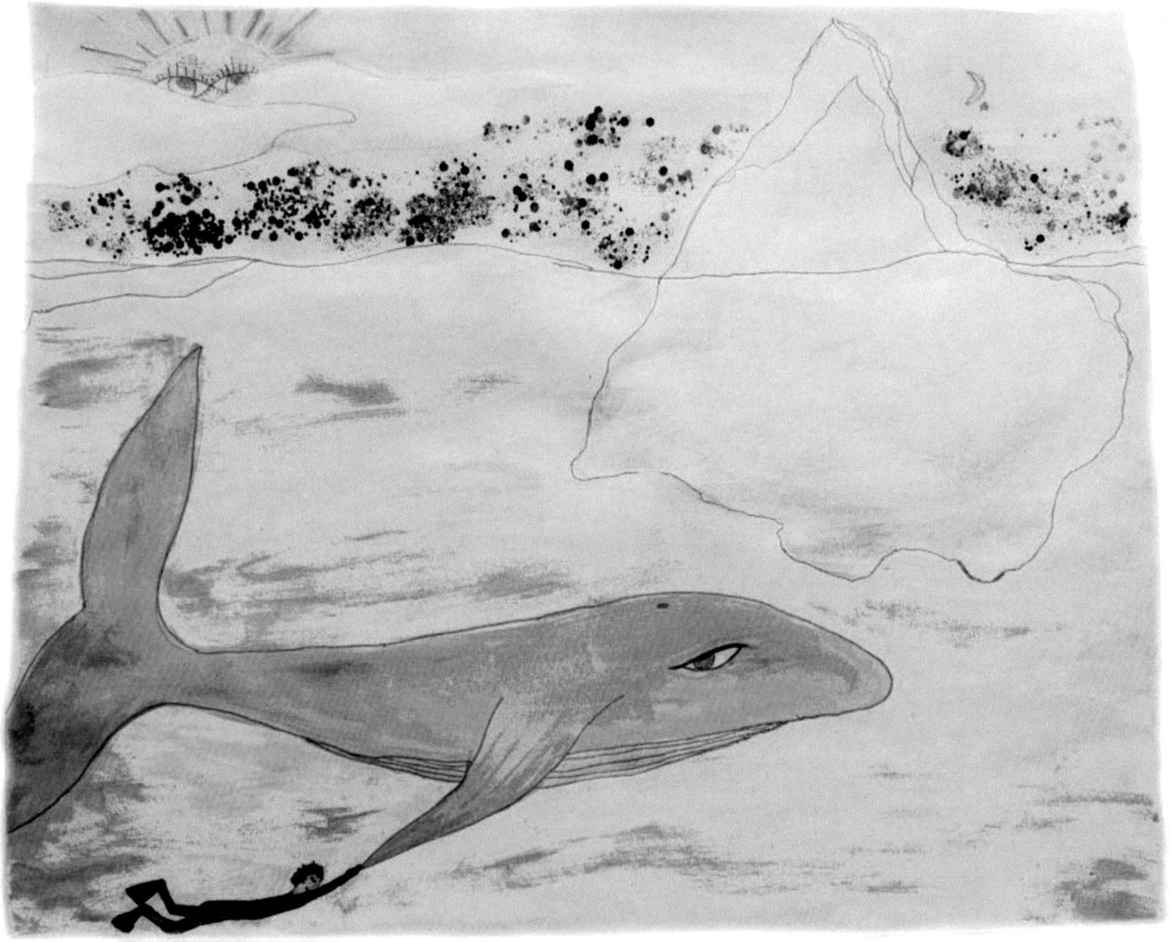

Just as a child
in a boundless dream
could climb mountains
as they slept.

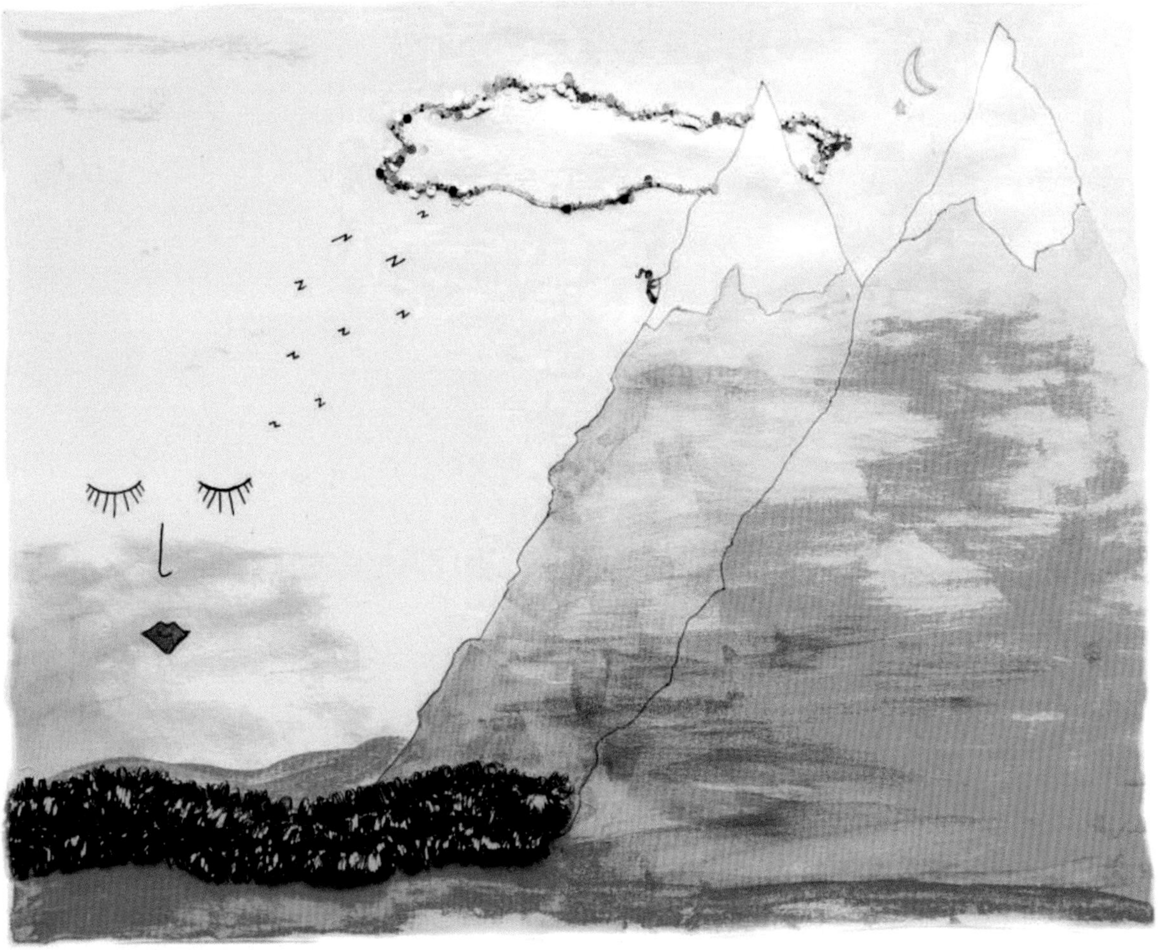

For you could be
whomever you wish if you
look outside the normal.

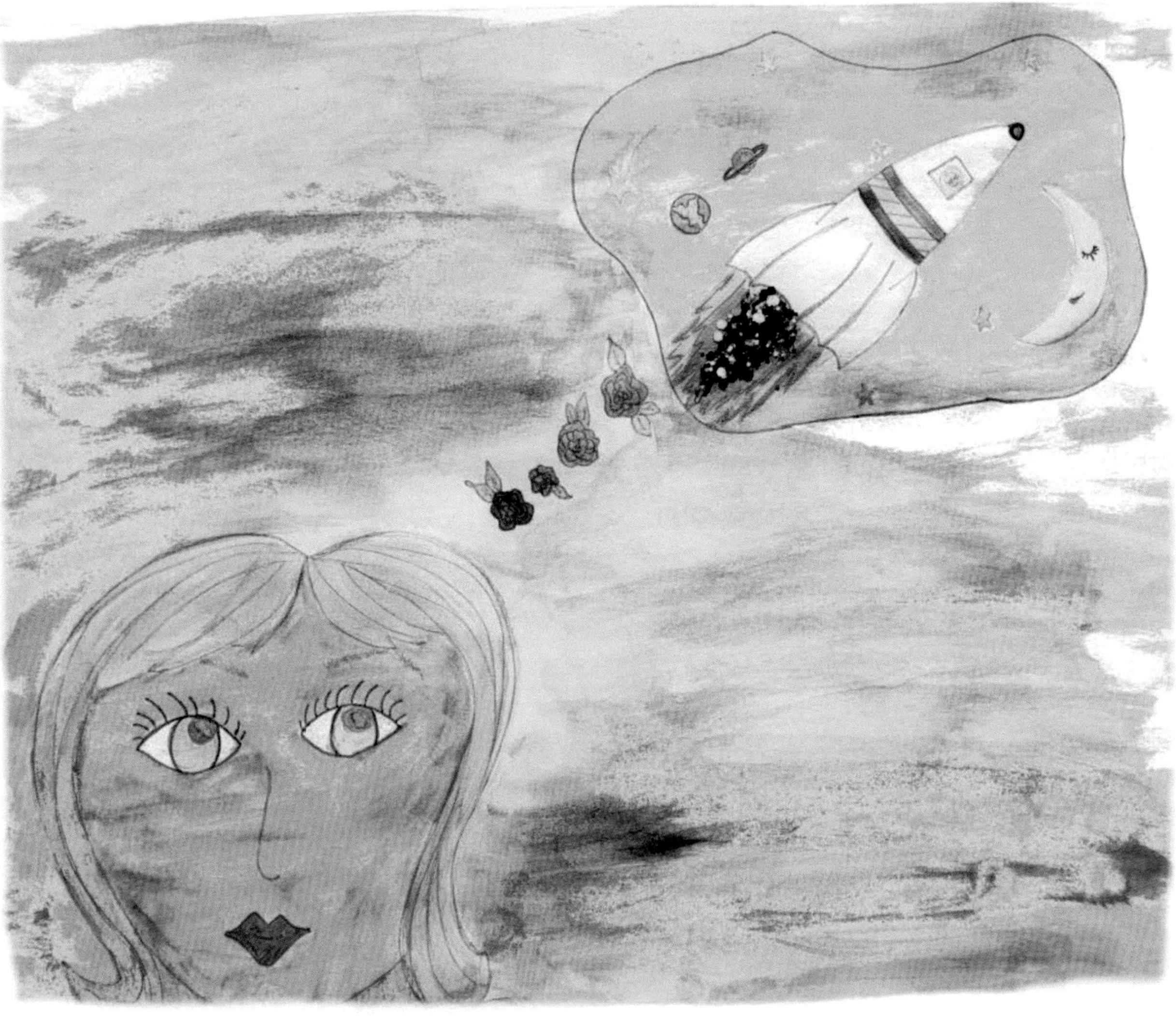

Craters can bloom roses
and stardust lives
within your own soul.

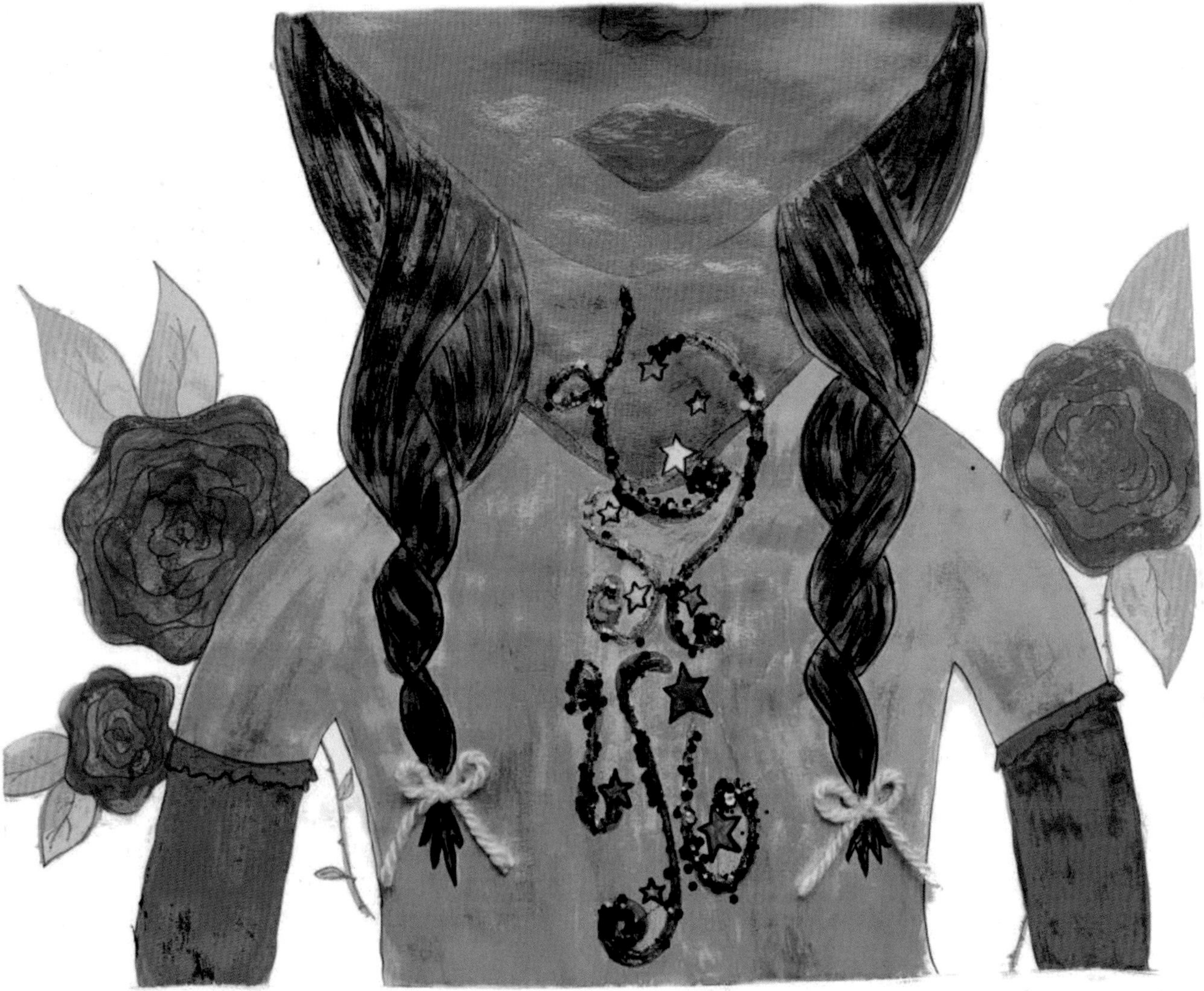

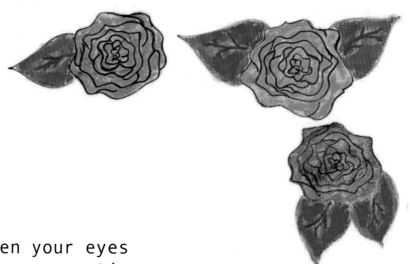

Open your eyes
to new connections
and do so very soon.

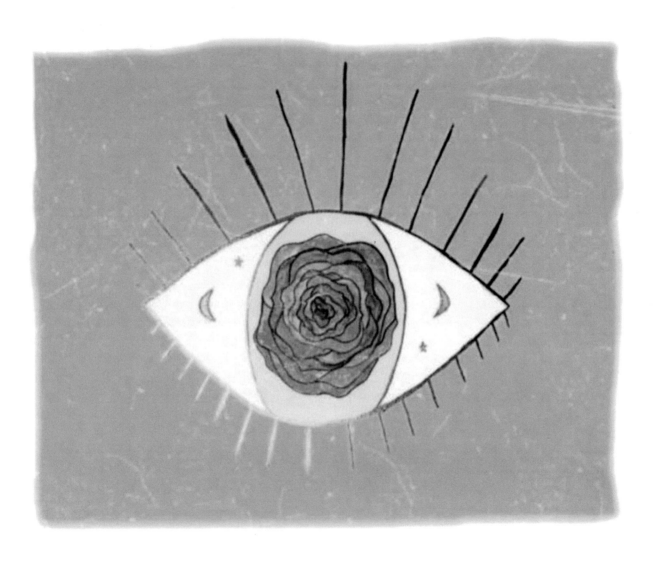

For you could be the
one who plants roses
on the moon.

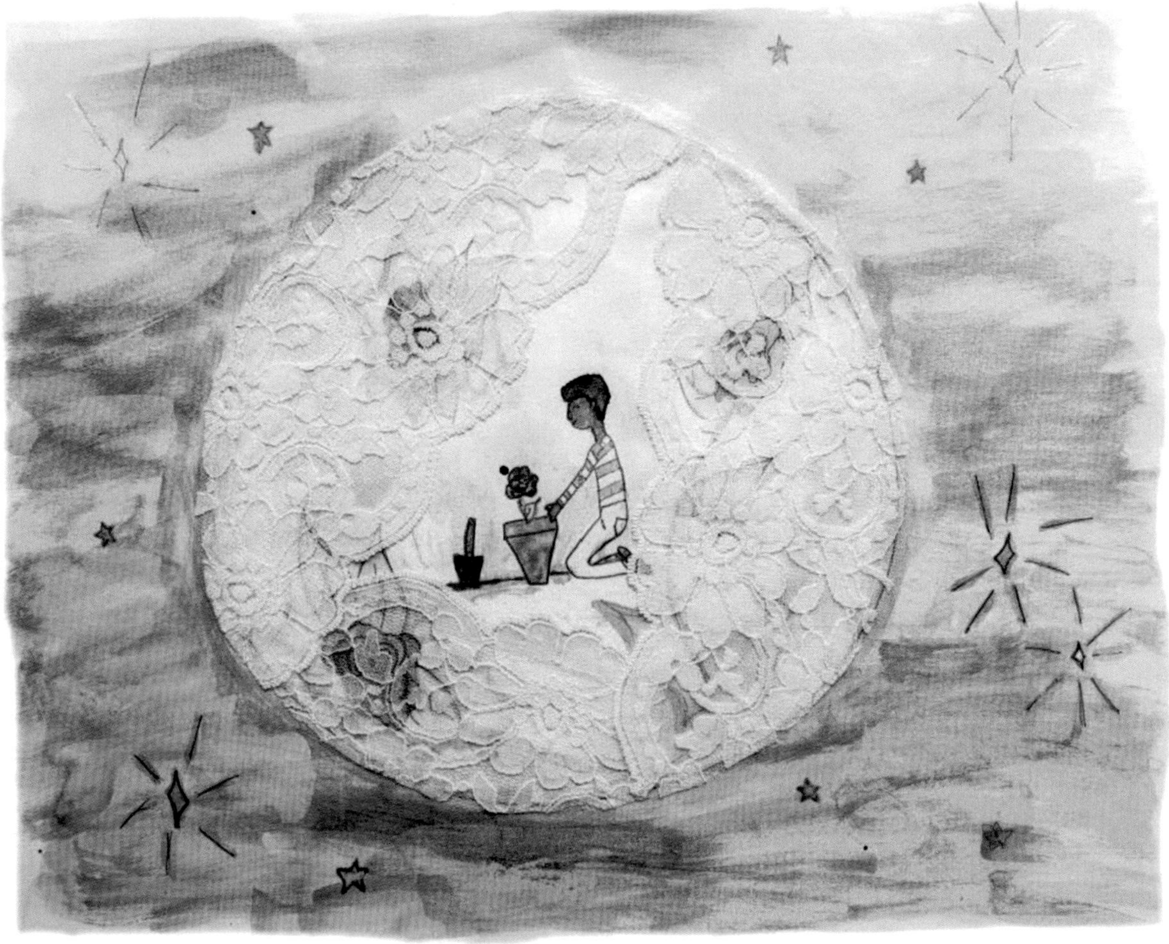

The end.

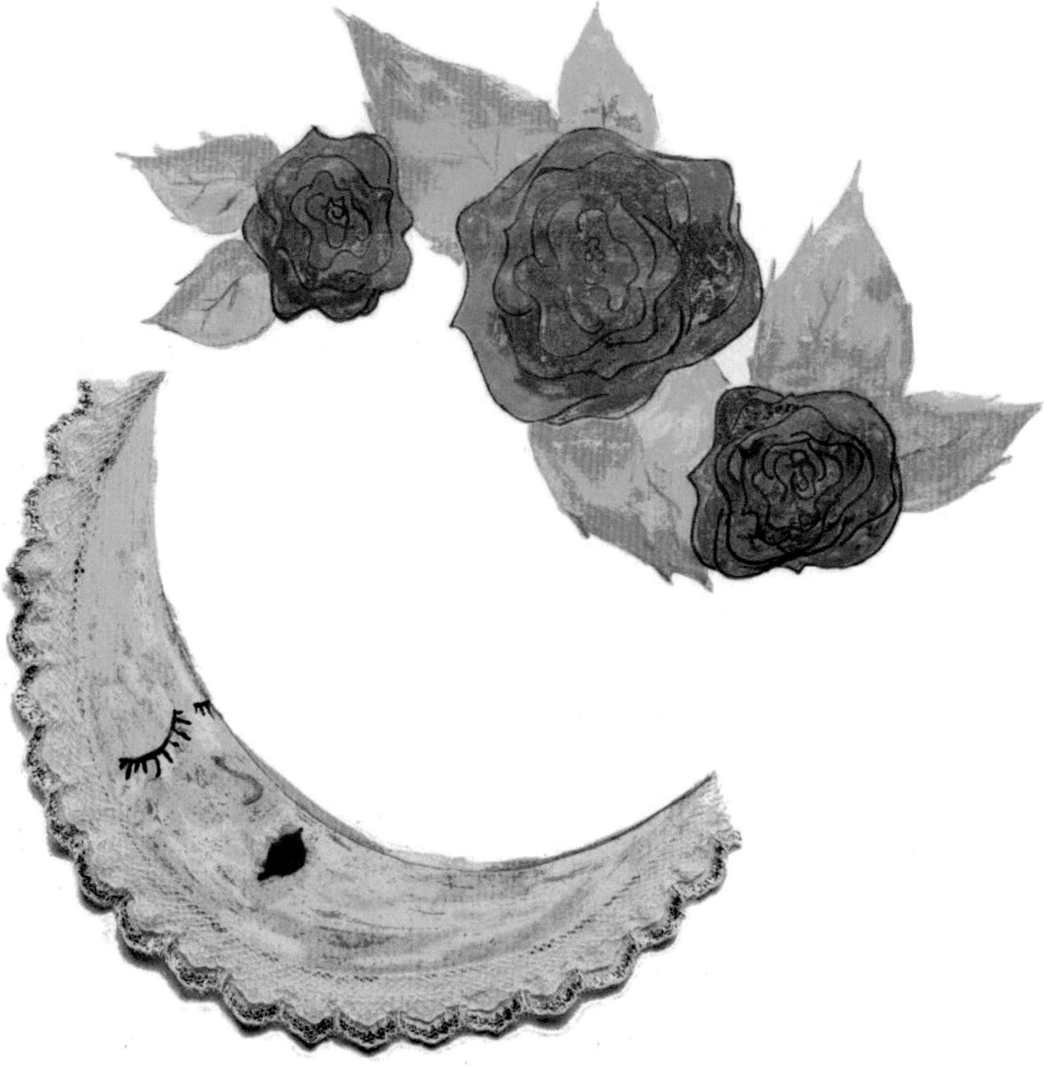

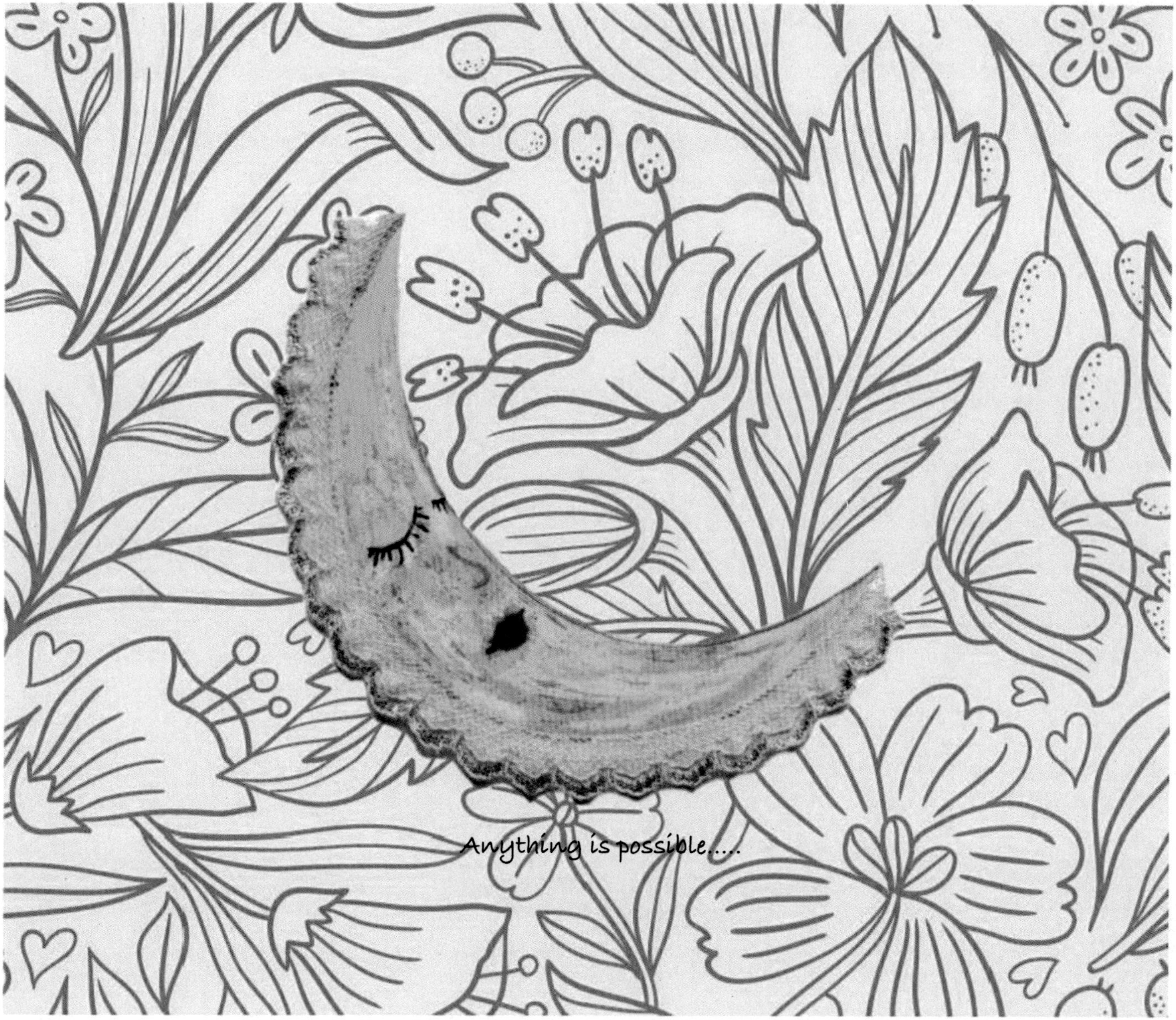
Anything is possible.....